1

Dedicated to those who helped and believed I could do it. Thank you everyone for the support.

Two Worlds And One Life: Bri's Revenge

By: Dawn C. Mackey

Chapter One

Flying in the sky, grasping her broom she swoops down to avoid the tackle. She blows by the defender, another one approaching; she swerves left then cuts hard to the right, faking him out. Just a few more yards and she scores. Flying up and down, left and right she manages to weave herself through everyone to score.

Panting she drops the ball as the crowd cheers and she lets out an exhilarating holler. They've won the game and get to continue on for the following tournament.

"Bri, you did so well!" exclaimed Beth.

"Thanks, I learned from the best! What's for dinner? I am starved."

"Well, you should be after that game of flying football. I'm not sure. Let's get home, so we can find out.

They fly home in a hurry rushing above the spellbinding town, particularly where the statue of Mr. Magi and Liz are with the flowing water fountain and scurrying people. Finally, they come upon the woods where the house sets quietly.

"How did the game go, Bri?" questioned Nana when the two landed in front of the door.

"Good. We won!"

"Did ya? That's great! By how much?"

"By one touchdown and I scored it." Bri replied back proudly. "I was dodging down the field and after I got past the ten yard line I was going to get that touchdown. I was unstoppable!"

"Good, I'm glad. You must be the only girl on the football team. At least the only one in history, who has done any good on the team."

"Yeah, maybe. What's for dinner?"

"You'll have to ask Eliza, she is cooking tonight. If I had to guess I think it is chicken but I'm not sure."

"Okay, well, I'm going in." Entering the house through the double doors, "Eliza what are you cooking?"

"Chicken. How did the game go?"

"We won. I got the winning touchdown."

"That's good. Dinner is done." Eliza yelled throughout the house.

Bri plopped in a chair as Eliza placed the chicken on the table. Others started to appear as well. There were rolls with butter, corn, green beans, mashed potatoes and gravy, apple pie and the chicken of course. It was quite a meal for a week day evening, but Bri supposed Eliza knew they were going to win. She had that kind of power of knowing things when they were going to happen.

After everyone was finished with their dinner Sara gathered the dishes as Eliza and Beth went to shower. Nana went to her bedroom to read a book she was just getting ready to finish. Bri went into her room and sat on her bed with the empty bed on the other side of the room, looking at it. She jumped off and reached for a box under her bed and pulled out a hand full of pictures. They all had Liz in them. One was when they were about seven years old they were in Liz's backyard playing in a sprinkler with Justin, Liz's older brother. In the background Liz's parents were sitting on the back patio watching them with her mother and her bulging belly.

Another was more recent, they were dressed in their dresses from the past Halloween, leaning on each other's backs and puffing their lips out to the camera as Liz held a red lipstick, and Bri held a blush container. They had this special look in their eyes, a look of pompousness and the likes of defeating whatever came their way. They weren't backing down look.

Eliza walking in Bri's room with wet hair and dressed in a fuzzy red bathrobe said, "You can take your shower now. I am finished and Beth is too."

"Okay." Bri was choking back tears.

Eliza came to sit by her side, "What's..." she stopped when she saw all the pictures of her and Liz together. "It's okay, Bri. I know it's hard and all, but we will find the killer and after that you can continue on with your life in Westward. The mystery will be solved and you know you'll always be welcomed here. You don't ever have to be a stranger."

Bri reached over and grasped her into a hug as Eliza patted her on her back in a comforting passion. "Now go take your shower and calm down. Liz wouldn't want you crying for her."

Bri gathered her bed clothes and continued toward the shower, knowing Eliza was right about Liz.

After her shower she started pondering, *there has to be a way Liz can come back. She is so strong and smart. We will need her to help us. Certainly she knows who her killer is now, right? Since she is gone, she knows the secrets of life now. I think. Maybe not. Oh I don't know.* She yawns as her head settles on her bright yellow, ruffled pillow.

Waking up the next morning she puts on an olive green dress that comes down to her knees, and a black band around her waist that ties into a bow on her back side. She eats breakfast, a bowl of cereal as Beth cleans the kitchen until it is gleaming in the morning sunlight. "I am ready to go to school now. Who will be attending me, you or should I go wake Nana?"

"No, I will accompany you. There is no need to wake her when I am awake already."

They get on their own brooms. to fly to the school. The school sets up in the hills, where the trees shelter it from the harsh weather, and it overlooks the town. It has a castle like appearance. The perfect gray stones that stack to create a sturdy wall protecting everything inside. The walls form a perfect square and at each corner there is a tower with a cone sitting on the top acting as the roof. Occasionally windows appear going around the tower all the way to the top imagining the spiral staircase.

    Beth and Bri landed, running some with the momentum they had. "Here is the map of the school. And this here is your new wand."

    "I think I can find my way around the school. Thanks, but what is the special occasion for me to have a new wand for. I think my other one was still good."

    "Well, for one thing Eliza scheduled some new classes for you so you will start those today. This wand will let you do more actions than your last one did. The map will be handy you'll like having Ms. Polenia. Also the new wand will be your closest friend, don't ever let it out of your sight. It will help with the adventures ahead but for now you must learn its power. What better time than to start now," she had more pep in her voice, "with new classes."

"Yeah, what better time?" There was sarcasm in Bri's voice but Beth just ignored it.

Giving Bri a little nudge to get her heading towards the school, "Enjoy your new classes. I know you will do well!"

Mumbling under her voice Bri responds, "Yeah, I'll do well."

As she proceeds to her locker, with her broom in her hand, she sees many other girls in the hall; she smiles to keep a settle between them all not wanting to cause any drama. There is an eerie feeling at the school; everyone thinks there is someone out to get them. Perhaps it is true but Bri doesn't want anyone to think she is after them. Who knows what kinds of spells and wicked things they can or will do? She arrives at her grey locker as she grabs her notebooks and folders to carry on to her classes. Her third period course is with Ms. Polenia but she has no idea what it will be about. The bell finally rings for second period to end and she is on her way to Ms. Polenia. Grabbing for the map in her backpack, she stops to read it. *Okay turn to the right here at the hall then make a quick left and up the spiral staircase. I must be going into the tower. I wonder how long it'll take to climb all those stairs. Well, I better start now.*

Entering the tower there is a monstrous spider web in the far corner, which dead ends and off to the side the steps start. They are a grey stone with a few chips and some cracks occasionally, but nothing too serious. Climbing the steps starting out skipping one at a time, Bri eventually starts to take each step as she starts to tire. *There is no way I am making this climb every day. This simply won't do,* she contemplates. Finally, after going round and round she meets the lonely door on her left side. It is closed. She knocks wondering if she is late.

"It's open."

Opening the door she asks, "Are you Ms. Polenia?"

"Yess, that's me," she speaks with excitement.

The room is surprisingly bright. Full with colors and paint! *Is she an artist? Am I in an art class?* There are easels and canvases all over the place. Some are hanging from the ceiling by a thin wire that is hard to trust. Some paintings are already framed and anchored to the wall. Bri stops looking around and takes in the face of Ms. Polenia. The sun is glistening on her face giving her a golden skin tone, like she is from the Heavens. She looks similar to herself with the defined jaw line and the high cheek bone. She has the same eyes but different hair color. *I know I have seen her before, but where and when.* It comes to her quickly; she has seen her in the photos at her house of her mother. Ms. Polenia looks like her mother.

"Why, Hello. Are you Bri?"

"Yes," she pauses and stares straight at Ms. Polenia. "Are you my mother?" She realizes how funny that sounds after she says it. "I mean… that is…you look like her."

"Yeah, it's me. How are you sweetie," she rushes over to hug Bri.

Bri still shocked, slowly embraces her as she does. "I thought..."

"I was constantly at parties."

"Yeah."

"That was your nanny when you were younger. She took care of you while I could live my life here. I know she didn't do well, but Nana knew about your talents and I told her to take you along for the ride. I didn't realize your nanny would be such a distraction. I am glad you're okay and a beautiful young lady. Now, we are reunited together but I don't want you to stay with me. There is important business to finish with Nana and the others. However, I do need to teach you some new things. Things that you can do that is special and no one else can."

"Okay, but what exactly is it? What can I do that is so special?"

"You can read other peoples' minds."

"Really, so when I hear voices sometimes it is really what they are thinking?"

"Yeah, I need to teach you how to embrace your talent and use it with caution."

The clock in the corner starts to chime, signifying the class is over.

"Okay. I have to get to my next class. Will I see you again tomorrow at the same time?"

"Yes and be rested up for it will be a tiring day for the untrained."

Bri starts down the stairs, going round and round as she descends. Getting dizzy and she trips and falls. Tumbling to what seems. forever comes to a thumping stop. She gets up quickly, while looking around to make sure no one has seen her. No one has and she continues to her following class, biology. Bri isn't too fond of biology she doesn't grasp the idea of why she would need to know the anatomy of a frog or toad but nonetheless she tried her hardest.

Finally school is over. *Should I go upstairs to Ms. Polenia, my mother or just go home?* She thinks for a while longer coming to the conclusion to go up. Hiking up the stairs once again she reaches the top to find out the door is shut and locked. *Dang it, I missed her. She must leave soon after I have her class. I wonder what she really does teach.* Bri starts her adventure home. She mounts her broom outside at the broom rack similar to the ones for bicycles. She takes off exploding into the air as if angry. She flies recklessly, swerving between other brooms and trees. Flying low to the ground to avoid tree limbs, she find herself pushing through bushes, making the leaves fall off, with her dangerous speeds; nonetheless she makes it home safely. Upset and excited Bri doesn't know how to feel. She has met her mother but why didn't Beth or Eliza tell her?

Chapter Two

Walking up the brick pathway between the flower gardens, carrying her broom and bag of books she ascends the stairs to enter the house. "I'm home!" She announces to the household.

"Did you enjoy your day at the school?" asked Beth.

"Yeah, I guess. Did you know that Ms. Polenia was my mother?"

"Yeah, isn't she great? She is a well rounded witch. Very good teacher too."

"I guess, I mean I just met her today, it's kind of hard to judge a person on the first day, isn't it?"

"Only time will tell for you I suppose. Why don't we go do something?'

"Okay what would you like to do?"

"What if we go broom paintballing and then stargaze."

"Yeah, that's sounds like fun. When are we going?"

"Now, of course!" Beth gathers the brooms. and out the door she dashes.

"Wait! Jeez, chill for a minute, will you? I haven't even put my bag down yet!"

"Oh don't worry I'm not leaving without you, silly."

Bri comes stumbling out the door, and then straightens herself back up before descending the stairs to mount her broom. They take off with a quick jar and before they know it they are at the paintball place suiting up in some protective wear. The protective wear contained a helmet similar to a bicycle one and put a plastic shield over the face; they also had to wear safety glasses for any splattered paint. There were thick coats to put on and a padded pant too, to keep anyone from getting bruises. Shoes were not provided however and it was the customer's job to bring toe covered shoes.

They pick up a gun and into the arena they go. Bri enters through a different door than Beth did to liven up the intensity. It was a stimulation of a jungle. There were veins left add right and tall trees that didn't branch out until at the top. The foliage was thick and it was a challenge just walking through it.

"I am going to get you Bri! You can run but you can't hide!"

"Well, at least I can out run you!"

"We'll see about that one. So you want to tell me where you are right now?"

"In your dreams, girl."

"Okay, I see you want this done the hard way."

"If that's what you want to call it?"

"OK!" They shouted back and forth.

However there were no animals present just a fake rain would happen to slow the fighting down for a bit. Hours and hours go by of Bri hunting Beth and the inverse of that too. Beth eventually got a good aim of Bri and let her have it. She managed to get the first shot at Bri just in time before their time was over.

"Ha! I told you I would find you first and get you."

"Oh really, you know I let you win. I have to study some stuff figured if I didn't let you win then I'd be in here for the rest of my life!"

"Oh, you are just full of excuses, aren't you?"

"Maybe!" They exit the pretend jungle and go out to eat and go just out of town to look at the stars.

"I haven't done this since Liz was alive. We use to look at the stars all the time."

"It's okay maybe someday you'll discover a new constellation up there of Liz herself. Then she'll be watching you as your watching her. Isn't that an exciting thought?"

"I guess I liked it better when she was here with me, but that'll just have to do."

They lay on the dewy ground a little longer before deciding to go home and then bed.

Finally the weekend is here and Bri can't wait to get away from school for a day.

"Good Morning Bri, how was your night with Beth did you have fun last night?" Eliza questioned her.

"Ya, I had a lot of fun. I haven't had that much fun for a while now. We went to a paintball place and then looked at the stars after. It was a clear night and they were easy to see."

"That's what I heard. Beth told me. I am glad you enjoyed your night."

"Yep," Bri responded as the conversation started to end.

"By the way your mother is going to stop by today and start you with some more training with your ability to hear other peoples' minds."

"Okay," Bri glances over to Eliza with an oblivious look.

"She has a lot planned for you today. You should have another fun filled day."

"Well, at least I have something to look forward to today."

As the sun is completely overhead, only a few gleams. of light find their way through the canopy of trees around the house as Bri sits on the front porch waiting for her mother to arrive.

In the distance she can see someone walking wearing a light colored green dress in which she suspects it to be her mother, indeed it is.

"Hey, Bri is that you sitting there waiting for me?" Ms. Polenia yells through the woods.

"Yeah, it's me," Bri answers back.

She picks up her walking speed and what looks like a picnic basket becomes visible.

"Are we going somewhere to eat?" asks Bri from afar.

"Why do you ask?" she pauses realizing her basket, "No, I have something for you."

"Oh." There is an awkward silence.

Finally Ms. Polenia is standing right in front of Bri, when she gives Bri a hug. "I didn't want to ruin your present so I decided to put it in something else. Go ahead and open it," she hands her the basket.

Bri embraces the basket tenderly trying to remember the last time she has ever gotten a gift from her mother. She decided she was too young to remember. Lifting up the lid she sees a little box which looks like it can hold jewelry. She takes it out and flips open the lid. It is a silver medallion of some sort on a navy blue ribbon. It has a heart on it that is elevated compared to the rest of the medal; with a single pointed leaf inside the heart. It didn't seem right having a leaf inside a heart, but it was there for a reason Bri concluded. She didn't ask questions just stared at it for a while then Ms. Polenia broke the silence, "do you like it?"

"Yeah," Bri didn't know what to say.

"It was your grandmothers, mine and now it is yours. You are the next in line to have it. You are just has strong as Liz was but you have one advantage that she no longer has."

"Oh, what's that?"

"You are still alive and breathing. When this is all done you can go back to living a normal life in Westward and see John again. The other difference is I'll be right by your side when you make the decision. But until then you have to solve the crime of Liz's death and together as a town we can do that."

"Really you will come with me; whatever my decision is?"

"Yep."

"Okay. Well, we can start by asking different people in town; such as the ones who work and live there."

"There's a start you and I will go together and we'll tell the others."

Peering through the door Bri hollers, "Sara, Eliza, Beth, Nana, come here," they come from all directions; "can you break into two groups and interview some people around town?"

"Sure, about Liz's murder?" Eliza asks.

"Yes."

They set out on their adventure, but before that they gathered some pen and paper to take notes. They asked simple question like, "What did you hear that day?" "Where you there at the center of town when it happened? If not where were you?" "What did you think of the situation?" And other questions similar to them. However, they didn't get much understanding of who could have actually done it. Everyone in the town seemed to be thankful of the defeat against the Harpers.

"We didn't make much leeway. What are we to do next?" asked Bri.

"Well, we can't give up just yet we had a couple that didn't even know anything about. They said they just moved from a nearby town. We had asked way they moved and they said they heard of a girl named Liz, but no idea she was killed," commented Sarah.

The rest of the night was silent as they all seemed to have their own thoughts on what to do and say the next time if there was a next time.

Morning finally arose and Ms. Polenia was still there. She had set up shop on the couch for a night; she was dressed and rearing to go when Bri descended the spiral stairs. The other four were all ready down the stairs as well. Sara and Eliza were sitting on plush chair reading a book as Beth and Nana were in the kitchen cooking.

"Good morning! How are we today?" Ms. Polenia communicated but it was verbally.

"I am good. Tired but I think I just slept too long," Bri said allowed.

Sara and Eliza looked over to Bri with a puzzled look wondering who she was talking to. They ignored it.

"So why did you sleep in so late?" Ms. Polenia asked her without verbally saying it.

"I don't know I just did."

"Bri! Who are you talking to? You are rumbling on and no one has said a word," Sara couldn't take the mysterious answers out of nowhere any longer.

"What are you talking about? Ms. Polenia asked me those questions."

"I'm sorry I was. I didn't mean to freak you out but I was seeing if she could understand me now using her power. She and I are stronger in the morning when we first wake up. It just works better. I can't explain it."

"Oh okay well I can't say if I was ever thinking anything in the morning before," Sara commented.

"Alright, now that you are awake go put on this dress." Polenia handed her a red dress that had grey netting on it to darken the color so it wasn't as bright. The sleeves just covered her shoulder and had a cap sleeve. However, those were the bright red, and there was a black bow to tie in the back; nothing huge just there. "How does it fit you?"

"Good. How does the medallion look on me?" There it was hanging from her neck. There was something different about it though, it was had a shimmer or glow to it. Not like glow in the dark type of glow but a glow with a white light like the sun's rays from above. It was eye catching and when Polenia saw her, she couldn't take her eyes off.

"You look beautiful!" she exclaimed.

They set out for a busy day. They grabbed their brooms out of a closet and mounted them outside.

"You know we should build a little shed for our brooms outside, like what cars have in the other millennium," stated Bri.

"Well, you can work on that when I am not taking you to town," Polenia said.

"I know but it would be a fun project, I think?"

"It sure would. I'll help you. We can start it tomorrow."

Polenia took her to town and that is where they practiced. Since they both had the same power she thought it would be easy to teach it to Bri.

"Here we are," they take a seat on a nearby wood bench, with an oak finish; "You can turn your power on and off. It is easy once you learn how so that is what you are going to learn. See that little girl what is she thinking. Can you tell?"

Bri looks at her not knowing what to do. Sometimes she could hear people but didn't really know they weren't talking. She just thought it was normal; she paid more attention realizing the child's lips were not moving. "I want candy." Of course a child's simple thought. She looks at Polenia and tells her.

"Yeah your right."

They sit there a while longer as she picks out people for Bri to hear their thoughts. Bri picks up quick on how to take control on what she does and doesn't want to hear. "Now just so you know you never want to be listening to others during certain circumstances, like for example when someone is thinking for a test. You understand?"

"I understand loud and clear on what you are saying."

"You better after all; I am your teacher too," Polenia tries to scare.

"Your tricks will never work against me!!" Bri exclaims, rising from the bench with confidence throwing her fist into the air. Others looked over wondering, "What is her problem?" but no one approached them.

"Will you sit down... you are a nutcase. You know that?"

"NO! Really? You are the first to tell me that," she reaches over to grab her broom, sitting on it to take off, "Never in a million years!" She is in the air flying.

Polenia doesn't know what to think, so she decides to do the only thing to do that is to chase Bri. She whips up into the air and weaves through the clouds and others who are flying. "Sorry, pardon me!" are her words in the air. Finally she catches up with Bri where they are just a minute from the house.

"Geez, girl! What are you thinking."

"Me think?! You are crazy, I wasn't thinking back there, I was just doing, living!"

"Are you feeling okay?"

"Peachy!" They enter the door simultaneously, hearing those in the house screaming.

"The wind it is too strong I can't hold on anymore!" Beth shouts as she grasp at a light hanging from the ceiling.

"NO! Get out of here there is a tornado in here! Or something!" Eliza exclaimed bracing herself against a wall.

"Awwww!" The winds swooped up Bri and Polenia before they were able to turn to get out. They were holding on the side of the door frame.

"What did you guys do while we were gone?" questioned Polenia.

"Nothing there was a knock on the door and I answered it," Sara responded.

The outdoors was like a magnet to the storm for it managed to make its way outside and just vanished into thin air. It had only one intended purpose and that was to destroy the house or maybe the people inside it, who would have wanted to hurt them?

"Well, that was weird to come home to," Bri said. "I think I am just going to go up stairs and relax maybe read a book." She scrambles up the stairs. She kneels on the rug and reaches under the bed Liz had once slept on. Pulling out an old box that is covered in cob webs knowing this was the one book that Liz loved to read and managed to work her magic better. She hoped to find something out on how to connect with the normal life in the other world, without being present, she once knew so well. She reads and reads, page after page. Finally, she comes to a section that reads, *Connecting to Another World Other than the One You Live in*. Grinning Bri shuffles and focuses on the flipping pages looking for a spell or anything that may help finally she sees something that catches her eyes. It is a spell indeed and it requires her to make up a juice of some sort but she isn't real sure what the ingredients are. It calls for grubble berries and ragolmelon. "What are those, I never even heard of those before," she whispers to herself.

She exits the room and into the hallway that is lined with pictures of Eliza and her sisters' relatives. She descends the stairs and enters the sitting room where everyone is. She goes to the small library in the house, so back down the stairs she goes where everyone sees her again. "Where are you going, sweetie?" asked Eliza.

"The library is that okay?"

"Oh yeah go right ahead!"

She enters through the double door and they shut with a slam after Bri is in there. There are books all the way up to the ceiling and a ladder is attached to the wall that can be swiveled around the room. A desk sat in the middle of the room and there was a random ink well sitting on it. Above the desk there was a light that hung down and had candles on it but the candles were not real for if they were the desk would have tons of wax lying on top of it. Gingerly she moves the ladder and places it where she thinks the encyclopedias are located and then carefully she climbs it waiting to see what the books will with hold. She grabs some books for they have layers of dust on them and there is a slot missing a book but she overlooks the significance of it. Setting the books on the desk as she descends the ladder, her feet meet the ground and she wipes away the dust with a quick swish motion and the dust went scattering on the floor. Shocked she sees that it is a type of book that contains pictures similar to a year book. She opens the cover and flips through the pictures. There are multiple pictures of people in which they seem to be part of an organization doing work in the community. She recognizes a picture of Nana and smiles when she sees it. She continues to flip through to see if she recognized anyone else. "Oh my!" she screeches. It was a picture of someone who looked like John Debinski her boy friend back in Westward. "Is that John?" she talks to herself. "There's no way!"

This man looks just like him and the same age too. "Why would he no look any different than what he does now?" She decided it was his grandfather but why would he be associated with Magi Town? She forgets about the grubble berries and the ragolmelon and continues her search over this mysterious, identical looking man of John. She looks for names under the picture but unfortunately there are none. She goes up the ladder to find more picture books but there isn't any more.

Chapter Three

With Bri stopped in her own tracks she carries the book out in the open and waving it to the crowd in the sitting room she passed through. Stopping, "What is this? Can you guys tell me about this book full of pictures?"

"Sure come here," Eliza says holding her hand out to take a hold of it. Bri hands the book to her. "Come, sit down. There is plenty of room right beside me."

Bri responds and sits down where Eliza was patting the couch with her hand.

"Awe these were the good ole days, weren't they Nana?"

"Let me see I can see that far," Eliza handed the book to her. "Oh yes it was. I remember that day vividly. Here in this picture I was planting some flowers that I grew, and they bloomed a bright red in the winter. I was so excited to see them in the winter I went there each day to see if they had yet. They did and they were the most beautiful thing I'd ever seen in my life. This was a club I was in, similar to what they call a Garden Club now but we got to make our own flowers. It was a lot of fun but eventually we broke up and went our separate ways once the Harpers took over."

"Well couldn't you start it back up now?"

"I could but I'm afraid I just can't. There is too much going on. Polenia do you remember when you were part of it?"

"Ya, I sure do. I was young though probably just turned fifteen when I joined. I remember making a plant that was able to smile with its petals. The petals were long and yellow and when someone was in a bad mood it would smile hoping to put the person is a good mood. I don't know how well it worked but I liked it. It made me smile, when I didn't feel like it some days!" She grinned about her last statement and looked back down then up again to Bri.

"Who is this man?" She pointed at the picture, who looked like John.

"I don't recall," Nana said looking at it. "Polenia, do you remember his name he looks younger than me maybe you can recall?" Polenia takes the book out of Nana's hand, "Why yes I do remember him, I think his name was Johnny. At least that was what I called him."

Bri just looked wide eyed at the picture giving away that she indeed knew something.

"What's on your mind Bri?" Beth asked as soon as her eyes widen.

"I know him," she murmured.

"Speak up we didn't hear you," Eliza said

"I know him that is my boyfriend. Well, he was before I came here that is. His name is John Debinski and he is a preacher's son. He gets straight A's and doesn't accept a B. He was the nicest boy I ever knew. He wouldn't hurt a fly even if it was a life or death situation."

"Sweetie, don't draw conclusions. I am sure this is his father or grandfather," her mother attempted to comfort her.

"Mom, I don't think so. If that is the case then the men in this family all look alike."

"It's been awhile since you seen him, perhaps the visual memory of him is fading."

"My memory isn't fading of him," her volume increases as she finishes her sentence.

"I think I need to go back to Westward and visit. Perhaps, I can talk to John, visit his family again, and be on my merry way back here. I can get a glimpse of his father and another look at John. So who's with me?"

"Well, I am certainly not going to stop you with this one so I'll come with you!" Polenia said wondering what the town looked liked. It had been over a decade since she last been in Westward. Would people remember her, or would she be a stranger?

"Okay, well I am ready. Just let me...," Bri goes to get the brooms and grabbing one in each hand she hands one to Polenia, "get the brooms."

"We should pack some clothes shouldn't we?"

"No way! We are witches we can make our own clothes in a heartbeat."

"No Bri we are packing clothes. You are not going to be using your magic in Westward. If someone found out who knows what would happen," Polenia was very stern.

Bri didn't argue back she just went upstairs to grab two dresses and was back down the stairs in seconds with a sack to put them in. "Okay I am ready now!"

They exited the doorway and Bri jumped off the stairs as Polenia calmly descended them. Mounting their brooms spontaneously they take off into the air. They arrived at the center of the town and was able to open the portal so they could appear in the woods in Westward.

"Where are we?" wanting to know the exact location Polenia asked.

"We are a little ways from town. Nana always leaves her car right over here," she runs over to the side of the stone wall and looks through the tree to see if she could see it. She sees a bed of leaves and notices something red glisten in the scarce sunlight that peeks through the dressed trees. "Here it is! Now, you can drive and we can get to town."

"Okay sounds like a plan," they both start brushing the leaves off the rest of the red car and the keys were still in the glove box. They put their brooms in the trunk along with their luggage leaving the old stone wall.

As they drove down the road Bri was giving her directions to get to town, and every turn and bump in the road Bri still remembered. Finally, reaching town Polenia couldn't wait to get into some of the stores to shop. There were long gorgeous wedding gowns with sequins she couldn't take her eyes off knowing she had no use for one. Driving along a little further there is a store with shoes sitting in the window. She had forgotten how much she loved to window shop with her friends when she was about twelve, before she moved to Magi Town. "John lives just past the town down a little side road. You can pull in there. They should still remember who I am even though I haven't been around lately. As you know it seems longer while we are in Magi Town that what it is here in Westward," Bri told Polenia.

"Okay, sounds good to me. Should I come in too?"

"Uh, yeah, I don't want to go alone. You can sit and talk to his parents and see if you know them. Get some information. Maybe and John and I will go and get ice cream or something."

"Okay I can do that. You know it's been awhile since I talked to someone that can't use magic."

"Just do your best, Mom. I love you."

They finally pull onto a road and were soon parked in front of a white house. There was a brick pathway up to the stairs of the front porch and on both sides of the brick there were purple and red and light blue flowers planted. They were all in full bloom and were striking to look at. Bri got out of the car and brought herself in front of the front door hoping John would answer the door. She rings the door bell and waits for a moment.

The door opens and Bri holds her breath for what seems like minuets were only seconds. It's John! "Hello, Bri! Where have you been? I tried calling you for a while now and I wasn't getting answer."

"I know I left the house for a while to find my real mother so I haven't been home and that was my main focus. I lost my cell phone in the pond when I was alongside it skipping rocks. That's why you couldn't get a hold of me. Are your parents home?"

"Yeah they are in the living room watching a show of some sort, not really sure what it is, why?"

"Well, I did find my mom! Can she meet your parents? They can bond while we go for ice cream or something."

"That's great let me go tell them. Come in and sit down. You're not a stranger." He disappears around the corner and Bri can hear the sound of them talking but couldn't make out the words that were being said. "Yeah, she can come in, and they can bond. My parents were shocked when I said you found your mother."

"Hi there darling, how have you been?" John's mom said as she approached her to give her a hug.

"Pretty good, it's okay for you to meet my mom. She's excited to meet you."

"Yes, where is she?"

"Out in the car let me get her," Bri runs out of the house to grab her mother. They both come in as Polenia follows behind.

"Hello, I'm Kim Debinski, John's mother. I might say you have a well rounded daughter. John talks about her all the time. It's nice to finally meet you. And Bri must be excited about it too."

"Oh yeah, she sure is. My name is Polenia..." they talk for awhile as John and Bri slips out the door.

They are in the car heading towards the ice cream shop, "So what have you been up to lately besides trying to find your mother?"

"Nothing, that's just it. John, I have a question, I was wondering who were you named after?"

"Me, I was named after my father just as he was named after his. Why do you ask."

"Really that is really cool! I was looking at a book my grandma had and the man looked just like you. I couldn't look away, I just had to ask," she knew she was lying.

"Yeah it was probably my grandfather then. I mean if it was a book that your grandma had."

"I understand what you are saying. What would you think if I told you I believe in magic?"

He was silent for awhile.

"Okay you think I am crazy."

"Well, I don't know I guess it could be real. I don't think it necessarily exists in this world but maybe another world somewhere out there," he glances up towards the sky.

"What makes you think that? What if there is someone in this world that can do magic?"

"Well, I would just expect the media to be all over it."

"Sure, I understand but in a small town like Westward, we don't even have cops.

There isn't much media around either so how would anyone ever find out?"

"Girl, I don't know. Why are you asking me all these questions. I haven't seen you in sooo long and you want to ask questions about me believing in magic?"

"Sorry I didn't mean to offend you; I just thought I'd start up a conversation. Well, how's school going?"

They arrived at the ice cream shop and ordered a large shake to share with a cherry to top it off. Bri ended up eating it for she loved eating the cherry off the top. They talked about school although Bri didn't have much to say towards it. After the shake was finished they went back home to see their moms sipping on coffee and talking.

"It was a great night; I haven't enjoyed my time this much in a long time. Thanks," Bri commented.

"Anytime, I always enjoy my nights with you," they both looked in the kitchen, "know we need to separate them," John said pointing to the mothers.

Bri laughed, "yeah."

They finally got the two separated and Polenia and Bri were on their way back home to Magi Town. They arrived in the forest, and Bri who was fading away said, "We're going back already!?"

"Yeah, I got a lot of information from her today and it doesn't take that long to travel back and forth anyways so we can just go back and sleep in our beds. Besides I like my bed better than any other. Don't you?"

By the time she finished Bri was already pasted out in the sit beside her. Polenia couldn't wait to arrive back and tell the others. She didn't want to ruin Bri's night so she didn't bother to wake her. She parked the car, carried Bri out, and covered the car with leaves again leaving the key in the glove box. Bri woke up and together they passed through the wall when it split open. There they were again in Magi Town. They flew home and they both went to bed to wait for the morning.

Finally, the sun rose and breakfast was made in no hurry.

"So I did find out some interesting facts last night," Polenia mentioned, "It turns out that they have noticed John having a stick in his room in which he is protective of. She was seemingly joking around about it and how it gave him a huge splinter when he was younger but I believe otherwise. They smoothed the stick down and it had an appearance of a wand. I think he is a wizard, Bri. You have to spend some time there. Say you moved back into the area and go to school get to know him again. Stalk him Bri. If he goes, you go!" Polenia was very serious about this. She had a huge hunch and it could be very true just like before with Paul Harper. No one knew what he really was, now look at him, he is lying in a mutant Venus fly trap.

"I don't know. I haven't been in the school for a year now and I don't really have any friends anymore, other than John," Bri fright.

"Bri! You were a cheerleader when you were there. You have to have friends!"

"Stereotyping or what?! Well, I guess some will remember me and I could hang out with some of John's friends too. I'll probably be at the church a lot. Just saying."

"Okay, pack some stuff and I can go with you. Is the house still there?"

"The one that was supposed to be my home?"

"Ya."

"I'm sure it's still there if the cops didn't quarantine it."

"Ha ha, funny. Okay I'll fix it up for you when we get there," Polenia assured.

They eventually arrive at the house. It wasn't in great shape and was clear that it was abandoned. The grass was overgrown and the shrubs were too. There were weeds growing between the cement pads leading up to the front porch. And on the porch there were bird nest up in the grooves alongside the house under the roof.

With a flick of Polenia's wand the grass was cut, the bird nests were gone, and a bird house was placed in the front yard with a feeder nearby. The weeds no longer existed and the house was looking pretty good. The door opened by the force of Polenia's arm and it still obtained the same boring colors white, gray and black. With a flick of a light switch and a wand the room was glowing with blue patterned furniture, a green lamp shade with settle strips, and the kitchen appliances were red, except for the white fridge.

"Okay here you go. I am going to leave I'll check up with you but I can't stay here. You need to do this. You got this," Polenia was back out the door in a flash. She didn't say goodbye or anything just left.

"Oh boy, here I go," Bri murmured to herself as she continued to review what seemed to be a new house. "I need a dog here with me." It was like her mother heard her from the distance and poof there was a dog. It was a golden retriever and had a pink collar on her. She didn't have a name on the tag so Bri decided to call her Elle.

"Elle, what would you like to do first? "

She barks with a jump in her step towards the door.

"You want to go outside? Okay come on lets go check out the homestead then."

They go outside together and Elle never leaves her side. She was surprised when she leaped around her. They walked through some trails towards the back of the property to see the tree house still sat in the old oak. It looked dilapidated and Bri didn't dare to climb up. After they finished the walk around the land they came back in to nestle in front of the television, and slowly drifted into a peaceful night.

Eventually, the sun rose and was shinning loudly through the sterling window. Bri didn't waste no time at all she jumped up ran to a closet put on some jeans and a t-shirt and a zip up hoodie to go over it. She got two bowls one for water and the other for food for Elle to have while she was at school.

The day was rather boring there were some new students there but all the teachers were the same, and remembered her. She hung out with John the whole day and never really learned anything. On her way home John comes running after her.

"Hey, Bri! Wait up!"

Bri stops and turns around.

"Bri I was wondering would you like to come to church with me for the rest of this week, the choir and I will be performing and I was wondering if you would like to watch the rehearsals. That is if you aren't too busy."

"Ya I would love to come do I get to sing too?'

"You can if you want! I can't say no to you!"

"Yeah right! I was just joking around. I will be there to watch. What time?"

"About six, sometimes we are a little early and other times we are late, so it never is six sharp."

"Ok well I best get home I have that English paper to start on and I will get my math finished then I will stop by," explains Bri. "Bye."

She continues on her way home and when she enters the newly furnished door, Elle greets her at the door with a friendly bark. Bri pets her and gets her more fresh water letting her go outside for awhile. Then she sets down on the couch with her math book on her lap. She finally gets it done and has a short amount of time to work on English before she goes to the church. She only finishes a page and then lets Elle back in. She then decides to head down to the church a little yearly and had a feeling John would be there too.

    She continues to walk through the town to the church that towered above all the little quaint shops beside it. It had one tower in the middle that had the brass bells in it that chime, ever so often. On both sides there are smaller towers that have beautiful glass stained windows. She opens the large, wooden, double doors to allow herself in and sees all the benches lined up evenly with a red carpet stretched down to the stairs on the other end.

Bri walks in with tender feet and goes to find the upper level of the church were the practice room is. Up the stairs she goes and to her astonishment she hears voices. "Everyone must be here already?" she whispers to herself. Just as she gets ready to holler for John, she hears him talking about a familiar term in Magi Town but not in Westward. She continues to tip toe to the room and the door is slightly cracked she peeks inside to see John holding a stick, which appears as a wand. Just then she thinks she has all the proof she needs, and smiles as John realizes there is someone at the door.

He puts the wand into his pocket, "Hello is someone there? You may enter."

"Hey John, I was starting to remember my way around. I almost forgot!"

"Well, you came early I can show you around if you need me to."

"No I am perfectly content sitting here in this room, waiting for the others to arrive."

"Okay, that will work too."

Finally the group got here and they sang superbly, there was the one person that always sticks out the most because her voice, itself is an angel.

She headed home after the singing was done and didn't wait to say goodbye to John. She was going to do the same thing again tomorrow to see if she can hear a whole conversation.

Chapter Four

Entering the house she runs to get the unique phone that allows her to contact those in Magi town.

"Hello," she knows immediately that Beth answered the phone.

"Hey Beth, John is a wizard I am almost positive. I really want him to come back to Magi Town with me and he could help me with this case. I don't know how to tell him that though. I do plan to wait another day to see if I hear anything more or see any suspicions. But I honestly am a little nerve wrecked about the whole ordeal," Bri inhales and exhales rapidly.

"Dang girl, breathe some will you. Well, I will tell you this never in my life did I tell someone who I wasn't sure was a witch or wizard that I was indeed a witch. You'd have to talk to Eliza about that. But either way what makes you believe he is a wizard?"

"Well, I heard him talking about the portal, the stone wall in the woods and was talking about going through it. There is no way that a mortal would say anything like going through the stone wall. I mean seriously! I really think he is."

"Okay well sounds like you're getting somewhere from your stay. By the way Polenia said she gave you a dog."

"Yeah I named her Elle; she is a beautiful golden retriever. You'll see her when I come back home. Is Eliza there?"

"Hold on let me check; I can't say I've seen her today." Beth searches for Eliza and of course she was in the kitchen. "Eliza, Bri is on the phone she wants to talk to you," Beth says as she hands the phone over.

Grasping the phone, "Hello Bri, how is everything?"

"Oh it's going good here. Listen, I think John is a wizard. I want to investigate for one more day to make sure but I really want him to come back with me, do you know how to ask someone who might not be magical?"

"Ah, well you have two options that I can think of. One, find out if he is a wizard and if he is then all you have to do is tell him about you. Or two, ask him right away and if he thinks you're crazy just cast a simple spell to rid of the most recent memory. That's all I got for you now. I am going to go, you can figure the rest out..."

"Wait, hold on..."

"Bye," Eliza hung the phone up.

"Dang it she must be really busy," she says as she looks at Elle. "What do you think about all this, Elle?"

She just responds with a bark. Bri continued for the next half hour working on English and then bed to find herself waking up to do the same thing as the day before. Once again it approached six o'clock, and she left even earlier than before to see what's going on. She can hear a voice echoing through the church and follows the sound. It wasn't in the same room as before and the door was not cracked open either. She carefully placed her ears up against the door to hear what sounded like John and John's dad arguing about something. She wasn't exactly sure so she slid down the door to the bottom crack where she could make out some words.

"Why do you need to go back to the town? You know I don't like the idea of it no more!" John's dad says angrily.

"I need to get another book to study those potions. I finished the last one and the ones you have are so old. They come out with new potions just as doctors do with new medicinal treatments."

"Okay you can go tomorrow morning, and then you better get back home before dark. You hear me?"

"Yes, I hear you."

"Okay get on with your singing."

Bri backed up from the door and did a tip toed run down the hall when she heard footsteps coming towards the door. By the time the door opened and someone reached the stairs she turned around and acted like she was walking up them looking for John.

"Oh hey Bri! I didn't think you were coming today too," John acted surprised to see her.

"Well, I didn't want to miss you all singing."

Bri sat there eagerly listening to the group sing but she couldn't wait anymore. She pretended she got a text, and then a phone call and walked out of the church to get back to her house. As soon as she opened the door Elle was there to greet her. Bri gave her a pat and then moved on to call Eliza. The phone rang. No one answered. Bri decided she was going to travel back to Magi Town that night. She locked up the house, and brought Elle with her.

They reached the brick wall, Bri chanted the wall split and then they walked through it.

They found their way to the house and no one was there. The handle on the door was busted off. Inside the end tables were smashed in half, the light bulbs in the lamps were shattered in pieces. There was cooked food that was splattered on the walls throughout the kitchen. The curtains were all shredded, some were just hanging on by a thread.

Bri was speechless she didn't say anything she was just flabbergasted. She looked down at Elle but she just sat down and looked at Bri.

"Who would do this Elle?"

Elle just stared blankly at Bri.

"I bet whoever did this killed Liz. Why would anybody ever want to come here and take five grown witches out of their house? It just doesn't make any sense. I'll just have to sleep here for the night and then wake up and go to the book store in the morning. I'll really surprise John. Unless he already knows? I doubt that though."

Finally, dawn broke and about an hour in she headed down to the book store. She entered the little shop that seemed bigger on the inside. There were the sliding ladders on every wall and the shelves of books were endless. Bri went over to the schooling books where John would come in to if he indeed was coming. Sure enough she rounded the corner and there he was holding a book in his hand reading the inner cover.

Bri's unsure what to do at this point does she confront him now or does she wait until later when he goes to leave the store.

With uncertainty she does what came to her mind first. Show herself now in the store. She starts out by looking at the books occasionally picking one up at a time; she then rounds the corner in the aisle he was in, to strike his attention. He's gone. Bri picks her head up with a jolt and looks around realizing how ridiculous she must look, she slows herself down. She she's him at the checkout and follows him out the door. He mounts his broom but he isn't flying towards the portal of Westward. Instead he is flying east towards the house she lived in for a short time when she discovered her powers as a witch. She mounts her broom and follows him at a safe distance. To her surprise he swoops down near the house and finds it a little strange. He dropped something and it didn't seem to faze him one bit. He continues on his path but starts to make a slight turn to start heading west. Bri follows but she flies closer towards the ground in the foliage to help hide her some. Bri whispers to herself aloud, "I wonder why he decided to fly over the house. He must know about me, and heard something about what happened at the house. She rushes ahead of him and goes back to the town and gets a snack. About a minute later she sees John flying on his broom getting ready to land.

He notices her and approaches her. "Hey there Bri! Is that really you?"

"Yeah it's me. What are you doing here?"

"Oh I just needed to get some more books to read. You know, got to keep up on those studies!"

"Yeah I follow you there."

"So what brings you here?" He asks with suspension in his voice.

"Oh you know the same thing really. I have classes here too. So I have to attend those as well on a regular basis."

"I see."

"So do our parents have a house here to stay in?"

"No. Does your mom have a house here."

"She sure does would you like me to show you?"

"Yeah that would be great!" He seemed more content than he has ever been in the past.

"They headed back from where they came from after Bri was finished with her snack. She still had her wand in her pocket. And she figured John had his with him. They got to the house and she started to show him the house and that's when something let out this huge puff of smoke. Immediately Bri thought this was an ambush of some sort when she found her way to John side she realized how erect he was standing looking down at her. Slow she realized there were two others with him. She noticed his parents on either side of him. They started talking but Bri was trying to catch her breath in smoky area, and didn't hear what they were saying.

"Well at least we can put away another powerful witch that lives in the area," John's father said.

"Good job son! We are so proud of you!" The mom said in the background.

"What are you guys doing?" Bri questioned.

"Girl you are not to ask questions. You are better off not to say another word if you want your beloved mother and Liz's family members to live," his dad spoke angrily.

Just then a cage that was about six foot tall and looked similar to a circular bird cage there were the five adults in there. Bri felt defeated as soon as she saw them locked up. She thought, "If those five can take care of three people then how can I a teenage that just found out she was a witch about two years ago defeat them?"

"Bri! Be smart girl you are the only one that can save us. Believe in yourself. Believe in Liz. She is with you. She'll help you. Embrace her!" Eliza shouted out to Bri.

John's dad shot her an angry look and then stuns her much like a taser gun. Bri lets out a slight scream.

"Now your next rather you like it or not."

Bri fought back by trying to tug herself away but nothing happened John's dad's grip was just too strong for Bri to fight back.

"JOHN! JOHN! How could you? What are you thinking? Don't let him hurt me! Please!"

John doesn't say anything.

"So who killed Liz? Which one of you did it?" Bri questioned.

"What's it matter to you. You'll know soon enough." He was tugging her hair and she grunted in pain.

"Tell me I want to know!"

There was no reply.

Bri takes a few deep breaths and works quickly. She remembered some of the training that Nana put Bri and Liz through before the big battle before Liz's death. She reaches for her wand and cuts her hair so she is free of John's dad's grasp.

She points the wand at him. "Leave me, my mother and Liz's family alone. We just want peace and I think Liz of all people deserves that!"

"I don't think anybody here deserves peace. Now you better get back over here."

"I don't think so."

Just then exchanges of wand colors were ignited. By this time John and his mother rode ahead to where ever they were going to take Bri. Bri's wand shot out a blue color as his shot out a brown color. They each held their ground and the colors collided, facing each other head on with nothing to protect them. Just then when all the power seemed to be taking the life away from Bri her colors started to change and there was Liz on her left adding a purple color. It was two verses one. One Bri's right her mother was standing there, Polenia, on her right it was Eliza, Sara, Beth and Nana. Liz must have let them out somehow. It was seven verses one now. When their colors started to overcome the brown Liz started to fade away and it was just the six of them. Eventually they reached John's dad and he pulled back and gave up. They circled around him but he had pushed himself too far with his powers. He drained the life right out of his self and just laid there on the dark green grass lifeless.

"What about John and John's mother?" Bri asked the others.

"I don't think they really had anything to do with it, personally. I mean I can't be for sure but I think they were living under his wish, not their own," Eliza said with a certainty.

"I can see where you are coming from. I mean after all they didn't stay to make sure Bri was going to make it to where ever he was trying to take her," Beth was trying to reason herself to believe Eliza as well.

"I don't know you guys I really want all this to be over with," Bri added.

"You see Bri, it is we know he was Liz's killer. Liz for sure came back she would only ever have came back to help solve her case for others to know," Polenia assured her.

"Okay if you all say so I believe you all. So tell me where did they have you guys all locked up at anyways and how did you even get locked up?" Bri wondered.

"Well like how he made it smoky and then stunned me that's what he did to all of us.

I was making dinner and we were all scattered throughout the house really. We just weren't ready for any of it," Eliza explained.

"Okay well where you at when you got in that cage," she pointed at it lying on the ground sideways.

"I don't really know. It was just this black room we hung in and every time we moved it was so fast that you couldn't even register where you were going."

"Oh okay well at least we are all okay. Right?"

"We sure are!" Sara exclaimed.

"Let's get back to the house and start cleaning up. Shall we?" Eliza said.

"We shall!" They sang.

Chapter Five

They cleaned up the splattered food, the shattered glass, fixed the broken door knob, and straightened up the living room. They took the curtains down and put up some new ones. Later that night the room was all cleaned up and they had a fresh helping of food in their stomachs to sleep on. Bri headed outside with a blanket and laid it on the grass. She gazed up at the stars searching for Liz. Beth came out and laid down beside her on the blanket.

"Hey there girlie! What are you looking for?"

"I was looking to see if I could see Liz."

"Oh well did you find her up there yet?"

"No."

" I can see her. She is right there above you." She points into the sky, "Do you see her yet? Right there! See that bright star there up ahead? That is her eye, particularly he right eye."

"Oh I see it!" Bri exclaims, "It really does look like her. I miss her so much"

"We all miss her very much Bri. You are not alone."

"I mean I moved on but she was my best friend and it's hard to let that go. I just wish I had another day with her, although, years would be better."

"Yes it would be, but that isn't the case so we just have to stay strong. Just think we found her killer and know she can rest in peace and we should be able too."

"Ya I agree."

"So what do you say we go inside and get to bed. Remember when I said we should build a broom shed? We can do that tomorrow."

"Okay that sounds like fun." They both got up and Bri latched onto the blanket to bring it in the house and up to their beds they went.

The sun finally rose and Beth already go the wood ready to go. It just needed some nails and color and then it was done. Beth did most of the construction, pounding nails in at every vertex of the boards. Once it had a shape Bri was all over painting the colors of the shed. She painted it mostly purple, thinking of Liz. Then the rest of the colors were collaborated into the purple. They were in swooshing swirls around the little rectangular shed and wrapped themselves around it. They waved up and down to the roof and back down to the grass line.

When it was finally finished it was a shed that had a thousand words to go with it. The colors were great together with the purple, blue, yellow, pink, green, red, and white swirled together. Beth put a lock on the shed so no one could break into it, and they all put their broom in a slot that was personalized just for them.

Eventually, the day's events returned to normal and Polenia and Bri got a little log cabin of their own not far from Sara, Eliza, Beth and Nana in the woods. It had a cute little porch with two rocking chairs and a table in between the two to put drinks on. Inside it had two bedrooms, a bathroom a living area, and a petite kitchen. Polenia continued to teach at the school, while Bri continued her studies there as well. Every day the two of them would walk home together then head over to Eliza's and the other three's house for dinner then Bri would study, and the next day would be the same thing all over again.

The End